W9-DGU-823

LAST DESSERTS

MEGAN ATWOOD

NIGHT FALL

LAST DESSERTS

MEGAN ATWOOD

MINNEAPOLIS

Darby Creek
A division of Lerner Publishing Group, Inc.
241 First Avenue North
Minneapolis, MN 55401 U.S.A.

Website address: www.lernerbooks.com

Cover photographs © Walter B. McKenzie/Digital Vision/Getty
Images; © iStockphoto.com/Marcus Lindström (background).

Main body text set in Memento Regular 12/16.

Library of Congress Cataloging-in-Publication Data

Atwood, Megan.
Last desserts / by Megan Atwood.
    p.   cm. — (Night fall)
ISBN 978-0-7613-7744-3 (lib. bdg. : alk. paper)
[1. Horror stories. 2. School lunchrooms, cafeterias, etc.—
Fiction.] I. Title.
PZ7.A8952Las 2011
[Fic]—dc22   2011000932

Manufactured in the United States of America
1—BP—7/15/11

To my parents,
for supporting me in every single
way, every single day. I love you.

Deep into that darkness peering, long I stood there wondering, fearing,
Doubting, dreaming dreams no mortal ever dared to dream before

—*Edgar Allan Poe,* The Raven

Ella's scream pierced the night. "It's horrible!"
Jasper, with wooden spoon raised high
to attack, ran to her side. He skidded a little on
his pink Adidas as he came to a stop next to her.

Cocking his head to the side, he said, "Oh
come on, now. I bet they're not that bad."

Ella grimaced. "Wait until you taste one."
She stuck a plain, slightly burned sugar cookie
in his mouth. Jasper chewed thoughtfully.

"Well, *ma chérie*, you've done better." He
swallowed. "But your bad is my good when it

comes to baking. Are you going to decorate them?"

Ella scooped the entire sheet of cookies into the garbage by her side.

"What are you doing?" Jasper gasped.

Ella couldn't resist smiling. She shrugged. "They're not good enough."

"You could have fed an entire homeless shelter. Scratch that—you could have fed an entire chorus line!"

She waved the spatula in her hand for emphasis. "Look, if I want to own my own bakeshop one day, I have to do better than this!"

Jasper sniffed. He threw an imaginary scarf behind his shoulder and stuck his nose in the air. "Well, if you are going to be catering any of *my* opening nights, I guess you *do* have to be the best, dahling." He sashayed around the kitchen on his tiptoes.

Ella giggled. If he had done this at their high school, she would have died of embarrassment. She was used to it—they'd been best friends since he stole her crayons in kindergarten—but she knew the rest of the school wouldn't be so forgiving. She spent a lot of her school days at hoping Jasper wouldn't do anything too embarrassing. Luckily, the rest of his drama group was just as weird, so Jasper managed to blend in somewhat.

She poked Jasper in the side and he ran away screeching.

Ella's mom appeared in the kitchen doorway. "Who is getting murdered in here?"

Jasper put a hand to his forehead and said in a Southern-belle voice, "Why, Ms. Ruby, I do declare your daughter is abusing me!" Now both Ella and her mom laughed.

"Jasper, how many times have I told you to call me Sara? You're practically family." Ella's mom noticed the cookies crumbled in the garbage. "Ella May, what have you done?"

Ella hated it when her mom called her by her middle name. First, she wasn't a kid anymore. And second, it was just dorky. Jasper was the only other person who knew her middle name.

"The cookies didn't turn out."

Ella's mom nodded her head knowingly. "Meaning, they weren't perfect." She locked eyes with Jasper, and they shared a look.

"What?" Ella said defensively. She hated it when Jasper and her mom conspired against her.

Shaking her head, Ella's mom turned to leave the room. "It's just, sometimes life is messy—it's okay if everything isn't perfect."

Ella grumbled to herself. "That's why I'll make it perfect." She felt grumpy now. "Don't encourage her," she told Jasper. "You're *my* friend, not hers." She began wiping up the table, making sure to get every last cookie crumb.

She heard Jasper stifling a laugh and whirled around. "Oh, my darling Ella. You are so *you*, and I adore you for it," he said. Then he picked her up in a big bear hug and twirled her around. She couldn't keep herself from giggling.

"**I** know what will cheer you up," Jasper said, licking a spoon that still had batter on it. "Let's go to the bake supply store and get some pretty decorations for your next batch of cookies."

Ella smiled. Even though she knew Jasper was bored to tears with baking, he was offering to spend yet more time doing it. She wasn't about to turn that down.

"Juju?" Jasper said.

"Bees," Ella responded automatically,

finishing the catchphrase they'd started when they were little.

The tradition had begun in second grade, after they'd already been friends for three whole years. They saw jujube candies for the first time and cracked up at the crazy name. They decided then and there that the two of them went together like jujus and bees.

"OK. You're forgiven." Ella lit up inside just thinking about the beautiful colors and pretty decorations at the store and the perfect, symmetrical designs she could make with them. "Let's go."

Even though Main Street was only a half a mile away, Ella asked her mom to drive them to the bake supply shop. The recent snowfall made it impossible to walk there. It was only the beginning of December, but Bridgewater had already had record amounts of snow for the year. As Ella put on her black boots and black scarf and watched Jasper throw his pink scarf behind his shoulder, she hoped the rest of the season remained storm-free.

Ella hooked her arm through Jasper's as they walked downtown. This slowed them both down enough to give her mom a good lead, so people wouldn't think she was with them. Ella had always been shy, but since she hit high school, she'd made a point never to draw attention to herself—for any reason. No one at school even knew she wanted to own a bakeshop one day. It was way too weird to tell anyone other than her best friend.

Jasper let go of her arm and ran to the little

theater, which would soon be hosting a town production of *Cats*. He stood in front of the window, meowing softly and pawing at the air. Ella sighed and laughed. She turned around and saw her mom standing in front of the town's department store, undoubtedly thinking of Christmas presents. Her mom wore a bright red coat and winter boots with little birds on them. Ella smiled at that, too. Fresh snowflakes twirled lazily by. Ella breathed out white puffs into the cold air. Ella had collected perfect moments for as long as she could remember, and here was one. She turned in a wide circle to take it all in.

And that's when she saw it.

The sign said Marta's Bakeshop. A pristine window display lit up the night in a storefront that had once been abandoned. Ella couldn't take her eyes off the shining window.

She moved closer. A large wedding cake filled the left-hand corner. It was covered with frosting swirls shaded in subtle tones of aqua blue with gold leaf and pink accents. On stands next to the cake were all manner of perfectly decorated cookies—angels, bells, gingergbread men—covered in sparkling edible-silver dots and immaculately brushed with icing. In the right-hand corner stood a modest but classy Christmas tree, gleaming with white lights.

Ella realized she'd gotten so close to the window that she'd fogged it up. She backed up and looked around to make sure no one had seen her. Jasper and her mom still stood in their own little worlds. Ella turned back to the window.

Out of the corner of her eye, she glimpsed a sign. Directly under the Christmas tree a neatly stenciled card read Help Wanted. Ella's breath caught in her throat.

Help Wanted.

She could help, all right! Her whole life had been only about baking and decorating cookies and sweets. She was born to help!

Squaring her shoulders, she grabbed the door handle and opened the door with a flourish.

A bell tinkled above Ella's head. She looked around the tidy bakeshop. A high, sweet voice floated from the back: "One minute, please!"

Ella breathed in deeply. The pastel colors, the soft lighting, the warm, inviting air, and the overwhelming sugar smell made her just a little spacey. She shook her head to clear it—she needed to be on to talk to this person. She *had* to have this job.

A short, slightly plump woman swept into

the room. Platinum-blonde hair curled around her ears; it almost glowed under the lights. She had bright blue eyes that immediately took Ella in. The full skirt of the woman's strawberry-patterned dress hid behind a spotless, scalloped-edged apron. Ella felt like this woman had stepped out of the 1950s instead of the back room.

"Well, hello dear!" the woman trilled. She looked approvingly at Ella. "So well dressed and put together, I must say. Many your age prefer those low-waisted monstrosities, those denim . . ."

She seemed to be searching for the word, so Ella helped. "You mean jeans?"

The woman nodded. For a second, an ugly look passed over her face. Just as fast, she smiled a big, beautiful smile and clapped her hands together. "Indeed, my dear, indeed! Now, what can I get for you? Angel cookie? Gingerbread man? Too young for a wedding cake, I assume." She winked at Ella, and Ella found herself smiling back. The woman was radiant. She looked just like one of the cookies she decorated.

"Oh, where are my manners? Mercy me, how unacceptable! I'm so sorry, dear. I'm Marta. I've just moved to this lovely town. And you are?"

Ella swallowed and tried to stop smiling like an idiot. "I'm Ella."

"Beautiful name, just beautiful. Now, what can I help you with, dear?"

Ella just stared at her, smiling, then realized with a start that Marta was waiting for an answer. "Oh, sorry, I . . . cakes . . . whole life . . . job." Ella took off her gloves and promptly dropped one as she tripped over herself to answer. She could feel herself blushing from her toes to her hairline.

She stooped over and quickly grabbed her glove. Then she took a deep breath and stood up straight. "I want a job." Realizing she'd practically just yelled her sentence, Ella tried again. "I mean, I saw your Help Wanted sign and am wondering if I could be the help." Her heart sank. She'd completely messed the whole thing up.

But when she looked up, she saw that Marta hadn't left in disgust. In fact, the woman looked very serious as she continued to study Ella. She moved slowly forward. With each step she asked a question.

"You have experience with baking?" Step.

"Oh, yes! I've been doing it my whole life!"

"And this isn't just a passing interest?" Step.

"No, no! This is all I've ever wanted to do."

"You have a commitment to beauty, perfection, and conformity?" Now Marta stood directly in front of Ella.

Ella said firmly, "Yes."

Marta gave a huge smile and patted Ella's shoulder. "Well, then, maybe this would be a good fit!"

Just then, the door swung open and Jasper blew in like a pink blizzard. Marta's eyes narrowed and she recoiled, like a cat hissing.

asper said, "There you are, darling Ella! What a lovely bakeshop—all these pastels! I swear, I blend in so perfectly someone may buy me accidentally!" Jasper's voice bounced off the walls of the small room and reverberated in Ella's ears. She shuddered with embarrassment.

Marta had backed away. She stood appraising Jasper. Her blue eyes turned icy cold. She looked at Ella. "Do you know this crea—I mean, boy?"

Ella looked from Marta to Jasper. She

wondered if she could get away with pretending they'd never met. She felt guilty even thinking it, but she could feel her dream melting away like the frosting in the display case. She nodded, but barely. Marta's eyes narrowed further.

Jasper, oblivious, tromped over to Ella and put his arm through hers. "Best friends since we were five!"

Marta took out a dishrag. "I see." Her voice was as cold as her eyes. "Well, the shop is closing up for the night, so is there anything I can get you two?"

Jasper shook his head and looked at Ella. "Just grabbing my little Ella here. Are you getting anything?"

Ella shook her head so fast she thought she might look like she was having a seizure. What she really wanted was for the floor to swallow her up. She whispered to Jasper, "I'll meet you outside. I was asking Marta something."

Jasper's eyes got wide. He nodded. "Baking stuff?" he whispered, like it was the deepest secret they could have. If she hadn't been so appalled, Ella would have laughed. Instead, she nodded. Jasper winked a big, theatrical wink and walked out the door.

Marta continued wiping the counters with quick, efficient strokes. Ella cleared her throat. "So, did you want to me to, um . . . ?" Her voice sounded small and unsure.

Marta looked up suddenly. "Oh dear, I should have taken down that Help Wanted sign ages ago. I was looking for help in setting up, but that's all taken care of! Now, would you like a cookie for the road?"

Tears stung Ella's eyes. She took a last look around the perfect shop she wouldn't be able to work at. She shook her head, afraid any words that came out would be shaky.

Brightly, but somehow with a cold edge, Marta said, "Bye, dear. Thank you for stopping in!" She waved and went back to cleaning the counters, leaving Ella to her utter heartbreak.

Jasper slammed his locker. "So, want to tell me why you're icier than the blizzard outside?"

Ella shrugged. The second bell rang; if they waited much longer, they'd both be tardy. Ella hated confrontation. Worse, she hated how she felt, but she couldn't seem to help it. She blamed Jasper for her losing out on the bakeshop job. The feeling lingered like a bad aftertaste.

Jasper stood in front of her, hands on hips,

head cocked to the side. His lips were pursed in an almost comical frown. Ella knew this look—he wasn't moving until she talked.

She sighed and fiddled with the combination dial on her locker door. Finally she closed it softly. "I'm really upset about that job, that's all."

Jasper clicked his tongue and stamped his foot. Ella checked down the hall to make sure no one noticed him. "Well, what do I have to with that?" he said.

Ella took a deep breath. She just couldn't tell him. "Nothing. I'm just cranky, I guess. I'm sorry."

Jasper's face softened. "Forget that old bag. You could outbake her any day!" Ella smiled. Maybe she could get over this and forgive him. "Now, go on to art class and practice your decorating!"

They both turned to get to their next class. As he ran in the opposite direction, Jasper yelled, "Juju?"

Ella smiled and whispered, "Bees."

She ran the rest of the way to her art class and barely made it in before the tardy bell rang. She threw her backpack on the big table she'd been assigned to and flopped on her seat, trying to catch her breath.

Ms. Jenkins breezed in, flowing skirts flying behind her, her crazy hair piled in a bun on top of her head. Ella adored her.

"Hello, class! Ready to make some art?"

The other students grumbled and shrugged. Ella knew what came next.

Ms. Jenkins singsonged, "I can't hear you!"

The class grumbled again, but now most of the students were smiling.

"One more time, class, with feeling!" Ms. Jenkins raised her voice and cupped a hand over her ear. "Ready to make some art?"

Now the whole class roared back, "Ready to make art!"

Ms. Jenkins smiled. "Much better. OK, it's time to—" The door flew open and Jamie Higgins sauntered in. Hair in a foot-high Mohawk and so many piercings she jangled, Jamie made her presence known in any room. Ella was a little scared of her, which was a problem, because they shared a table.

"And then Jamie decided to join us," Ms.

Jenkins said.

Jamie's mouth twisted in a grin. "Sorry, Ms. J."

Jamie noisily made her way to the table, then dumped her bag down directly in front of Ella. As Jamie scooted her seat in, the metal legs scraped against the floor. Ella cringed.

Ms. Jenkins went on. "So, we're giving ourselves a break today from composition and will be working on free painting. Anyone know what I mean?"

The room was silent. "What I mean is you can draw whatever you'd like. We've been studying all types of form, but as we near the holiday break, I want to give you a chance to go wild! Access your inner craziness and draw whatever comes to mind. Let it flow. . . ."

Ella didn't like it when things "flowed." She liked it when things were contained.

Ms. Jenkins said, "OK, go!"

Ella stared at her blank sketchpad. Jamie scratched away in the next chair. Ella tapped her pencil on the desk and tried to brainstorm. Finally she started sketching a cake and thinking about how she would decorate it. By the time she got to the third tier, she was so absorbed she didn't realize that the scribbling next to her had stopped.

Jamie stared at her drawing, one pierced eyebrow raised. "A cake? We can draw whatever we want, and you draw a cake?"

Ella threw her arms on the sketch and shrugged. "I couldn't think of anything else." No way would she tell Jamie that baking was all she thought about. Way too lame.

Jamie snorted. "Right. I can't stop thinking of things I want to draw. See?"

Ella peeked at her pad. One corner held a dark angel, messy lines smudging into shapeless features. In the center of the paper, what looked like a haunted mansion sprawled out, complete with crooked lines and oddly shaped details.

All around the edges of the paper, little doodles of gargoyles and vampires stared through their messy outlines. Jamie's hands were black from the charcoal she'd used.

Ella guessed the drawings were good, but they were way too messy for her taste. Not one line stood straight!

Ms. Jenkins leaned in to peer at Jamie's work. "Fantastic, Jamie! Your sense of distorted space is superb. I like how you've indicated the warp of time and reality with those asymmetrical lines."

Ella blinked. *She got all that from a gargoyle?*

Ms. Jenkins went on. "Let's see yours, Ella." She looked over Ella's drawing.

"Wow, two more different table partners couldn't be found. Ella, your sense of symmetry and proportion are beautiful, but . . ."

Ella looked up at her, brow furrowed. Hers was way better than the mess Jamie had made.

"But . . . I would love to see you go a little crazy here. You were given the freedom to draw whatever you wanted, and you went for straight, clean lines. Don't you think you could take a risk and try to draw something new?" Ms. Jenkins's eyes had gone soft.

Ella could feel herself blushing again. She was afraid to look around and see if anyone was looking at her. She nodded and looked down at the table.

Ms. Jenkins patted her shoulder. "Don't get

me wrong, you've got great talent. I'd just like to see you get a little messy is all." Ella looked up. Ms. Jenkins winked and went on to the next student. Ella's mother's words rang in her ears: "Sometimes life is a little messy." She sighed.

Ella could feel Jamie's eyes on her, so she turned to look at her.

"Dude," said Jamie, "you're über uptight." Jamie leaned in and tugged on Ella's brown hair. "Gotta loosen up a little!" Ella stiffened and Jamie laughed.

She had never been so happy to hear the bell ring for lunch in her life.

Ella was pretty sure her day couldn't get any worse. She flopped onto a seat across from Jasper at lunchtime.

Jasper looked up from the takeout sushi in front of him. "What's going on?"

Ella rolled her eyes. "Ugh. Ms. Jenkins said I was a bad artist." She put her head on her arms and sighed.

Jasper raised one eyebrow dramatically. "She actually *said* you were a bad artist?"

Ella grumbled. "Well, not exactly. She just

loved what freaky Jamie was doing, which, if you ask me, was like a seizure on paper. And then she said I needed to get messy. That my lines were 'too clean' and I needed to 'loosen up a little.'"

Jasper almost choked on his sushi. "You? That's like asking a zebra to change to polka dots!"

For some reason, this made Ella mad. At least she didn't dress like a crazy person and quote old movies all the time. Oh yeah, and wear pink Adidas while being a guy. And, the kicker, ruin her best friend's chance at her dream job.

"Whatever," she said, jumping up. She'd forgotten her lunch, so she needed to get food in the lunch line anyway.

Jasper shook his head. She could hear him say as she walked away, "Moody, moody."

Standing in line, Ella knew she was being unfair. She would apologize to Jasper when she sat down. He didn't deserve this treatment. But she had to admit—she still blamed him for her missed opportunity. If he was just more normal . . .

By the time the lunch lady plopped some gluelike macaroni and cheese on her plate, Ella felt completely confused. She grabbed an apple and some milk and went to pay for the food.

And that's when she saw them.

Perfectly decorated angel and gingerbread cookies sat in a perfectly decorated basket. The mixed chocolate and white cookies looked more like tiny cakes than cookies. Silver bells and thin icing graced their tops—they were just like the ones Ella had seen in the window. Each package was wrapped in cellophane and had a blue-and-white ribbon tied in a perfect bow around it.

The hand-stenciled writing on the sign said, "Marta's Cookies. $1.00 for 6."

Ella clenched her fists. That woman managed to get her cookies sold here? And why was she charging so little? Now everyone would be eating them. She looked around. Sure enough, almost every student carried a cellophane package with a blue-and-white bow.

Ella took out her wallet to pay for her food. The cashier said, "Would you like some cookies? They're brand-new and so cheap!" Ella didn't even answer. She practically threw her money at the cashier to get out of there as fast as she could. The cashier raised her eyebrows and handed Ella her change.

Ella stomped back to her table. She slammed the tray down and looked up at Jasper. He had one of the cookies halfway to his mouth. Ella slapped it out of his hand. The angel broke in half on the table.

"Have you gone mad?" Jasper said. "I know this is a bit off my diet, but good god, girl! You've ruined a perfectly good cookie!"

Ella rolled her eyes at him again. "Did you actually read the sign?"

Jasper shrugged. "The sign?"

"For the cookies! When you bought them! The cookies are from Marta's!"

Jasper looked bewildered. "Who's Marta?"

Ella growled again. "That woman who wouldn't give me the job. From last Saturday?"

"Oh. That Marta. And that means . . . ?"

Ella couldn't believe Jasper was acting this way. She waited a minute to see if he'd get it, but he just kept looking at her expectantly. She sighed, exasperated. "And that means you can't eat the cookies."

Jasper looked longingly at the broken angel. "Because you're my friend, and we're boycotting the shop," he said, sighing.

Ella sat back. "Exactly." She didn't mention that he also was the reason she didn't get the job and that he should be denied the cookies as a punishment.

Jasper squared his shoulders and looked up. "Right. Plus, these cookies clearly suck. Who would decorate an angel blue? Everyone knows they should be pink." He smiled and winked at Ella. She knew he was just trying to make her feel better. But the angels *were* beautiful, and just the smell from the broken cookie on the table made Ella's mouth water. Jasper kept looking at the cookie as if it were a long-lost brother. Ella could only image how good his tiny taste had been. Jealousy flared up in Ella, but with it came an appreciation for her oldest friend's loyalty.

Ella smiled. "Juju?"

"Bees. Most definitely," Jasper answered.

As the days passed, it seemed more and more people were talking about Marta's cookies. Ella did her best to put her bad feelings behind her. So what if a new bakeshop completely foiled her plan to be the best baker in town? And so what if that bakeshop owner wouldn't hire her? And so what if she felt it was her best friend's fault?

With the new bakeshop as her competition, Ella decided she needed to adapt. So when the bell rang for art class a few days later, she tried to think messy. Maybe she could draw some crazy lines like Jamie did.

When she got to class, she was surprised to see Jamie in her usual seat—on time. Jamie's Mohawk was gone, too. She wore her hair down like a normal person, although it was still blue. Ella sat down on her chair and stared at Jamie.

When Jamie noticed her looking, Ella jumped. But all Jamie did was say, "Yes?" in a polite voice.

Very weird.

Ms. Jenkins breezed in when the bell rang, wearing a long, straight skirt and a tucked-in blouse. Ella shifted in her seat.

"OK, class, we'll stay with the original lesson plan. Draw what you'd like." And then she stopped. Ella imagined she'd do her usual art chant. Instead, Ms. Jenkins said, "Oh, but do try to make it pretty, yes?"

Ella shook her head to clear it. *Pretty?*

Shrugging the strangeness off, Ella began to draw. She drew her normal, three-tiered cake, but this time she drew some fuzzy lines around the edges to make it look more abstract. When she was done, she held the paper in front of her to get a better perspective.

She couldn't believe her eyes. The messy lines made the cake much more interesting to look at. She would have never thought! She couldn't wait to show Ms. Jenkins.

Just then, she felt a presence behind her.

"What happened, dear?"

Ella swiveled her neck around. "What do you mean?"

Ms. Jenkins pressed her hand on Ella's shoulder. Ella tried to shake off Ms. Jenkins's grip. The teacher's voice got hard. "I mean, why did you put those horrible lines over that beautiful cake?"

Speechless, Ella just stared at her. Ms. Jenkins's fingers dug into her shoulder, and Ella said softly, "Ms. Jenkins, you're hurting me."

Ms. Jenkins seemed to shake something off. She patted Ella's shoulder. "Oh, I'm so sorry." Ella could see her eyes now. They looked like a cloud was lifting. Ms. Jenkins swallowed, then leaned down to Ella's drawing again. "Yes, yes, I love what you've done here. You've made real progress." She cleared her throat, gave Ella one last pat, and moved on.

Ella rubbed her shoulder and watched Ms. Jenkins make her way around the room. What had just happened?

She turned to Jamie. Maybe she'd noticed. "Do you think Ms. Jenkins is acting weird?" Ella whispered.

Jamie looked up with wide eyes, her face serene. She shook her head. "No, I don't believe so."

Ella stopped. Tattooed, pierced Jamie had just said, "No, I don't believe so."

Jamie looked over at Ella's drawing. "That's very nice, except for the lines. Here, look at mine."

Ella took in the drawing. On the paper, a still life of flowers, fruit, and bread graced the center, all the lines neat and orderly.

Jamie said to her, "See how perfect this is? Why make art if not to make things look improved?"

Ella slid onto a chair at the lunch table.

"OK," she said. "This is a very strange day. Do you think something's up?"

Jasper patted Ella's hand. "Do remember, *ma chérie*, that I'm not actually in your head with you. What are you going on about?"

Ella rolled her eyes at him. "Jasper, focus. Has anything strange happened to you today?"

The crinkle of cellophane and the "aaahs" of people eating cookies reached Ella's ears. She tried to tune them out. It worked. Mostly.

Jasper picked up a sushi roll with his chopsticks and ate it in one bite. Still chewing, he said, "No, why? Did you suddenly decide to color outside the lines?" He chuckled, and a piece of rice flew onto the table. Ella ignored the urge to wipe it away with a napkin.

Ella sat up straighter. "Actually, I did."

Jasper's eyebrows arched. "You did?"

"Yes, but that's not the strangest thing."

"Oh, do tell." Jasper put down his chopsticks.

"Ms. Jenkins was acting really weird in art class. And Jamie, my table partner, had her hair down."

"Oh no! Someone is having a bad day, and another person changed her hair? Has the whole world gone mad?"

Jasper's shouts brought hard stares from other tables. Ella wished the floor would open up. But Jasper just looked at her, amused.

"If you're not catching on, I'm being sarcastic."

"Yes, I got that, thank you very much. But just keep your eye out."

Jasper said, "I'll keep two out. So! Now I

have news to tell you—guess who's auditioning for *Cats*?"

Ella opened her lunch and took out her sandwich, cut in two perfect halves. She half-listened to Jasper as she looked around for other strange behavior.

Jasper went on, "Moi! Actually, our whole drama club is going to audition. We hope to make the chorus. Actually, actually," he leaned in closely, "I hope to be the star. But don't tell anyone that." He put a finger to his lips.

Ella nodded and chewed her sandwich, looking around. "Uh huh." She did notice the lunchroom was quieter than normal—except for the crinkle of the cellophane. It seemed everyone had the cookies now. She clenched her jaw.

Jasper snapped his fingers in front of her. "Hellooooo. Let's practice our listening skills today, shall we?"

Ella looked up guiltily. "Sorry."

Just then Carlos Perez, Bridgewater High's starting quarterback, walked by. His hair was parted on the side and gelled in place. Ella stared. He was one of the most popular kids at school, but today he looked so . . . dorky. He tripped and ran into Jasper.

Ella braced herself for the confrontation. The football team never missed an opportunity to make fun of Jasper. But Carlos only said, "Oh, excuse me," and patted Jasper on the shoulder.

Ella and Jasper looked at each other, astonished.

"OK, I'm with you now," Jasper said. "Something really weird is going on at Bridgewater High."

When she woke up the next morning, Ella hoped she had imagined everything. She'd tried to tell her mom that things had gotten weird at school, but came up short on any reasons why. Her mom had only said, "Sounds like you're overreacting, honey. Cookie?" When she'd held up a beautifully decorated angel cookie from Marta's, Ella had stomped away.

Ella reached her locker, but Jasper wasn't at his. She looked around. The school seemed even weirder than the day before.

The students walked around quietly. Boys' hair was parted neatly; girls' hair was smoothed down and flipped up at the ends. Nearly every single student wore a cardigan. An honest-to-god cardigan. What was going on?

As she entered homeroom, the strangeness got even stranger. Every single student looked directly at her and stared. *Glared.*

Ella sunk lower and lower in her seat. That's when she noticed another student without a cardigan: Rash. Her real name was Rachel, but everyone called her Rash because of her horrible food allergies. Was it possible both she and Rash had missed an announcement about some school pride day involving cardigans?

She couldn't wait to see Jasper. When the bell rang she fled to her locker, but Jasper still wasn't in.

"Of all the days," she whispered to herself. Trying to seem inconspicuous, almost climbing into her locker, Ella prayed for art class. Maybe Ms. Jenkins had some idea about what was going on. Ella didn't have a good feeling about any of it.

Finally, the bell rang. Ella practically sprinted down the hall. She arrived first and bounced in her seat. The rest of the class trickled in, each student wearing a cardigan, hair uniform and neat.

Jamie sat next to her and glared. All her piercings were gone. Her hair was mousy brown.

Ella cleared her throat and tried to ignore Jamie's eyes. Finally, she couldn't stay quiet any longer. "What?" she asked, her voice three octaves higher than normal.

Jamie pasted a smile on her face, but her brown eyes still held the anger. "Oh, golly, was I staring?"

Ella couldn't answer. *Golly?*

Jamie went on. "I was just . . . admiring your outfit. It's very . . . revealing."

Ella looked down at her own V-neck argyle sweater and jeans. She didn't have time to dwell because Ms. Jenkins walked in with short, choppy steps. The heels she wore seemed to hinder her steps.

Ella did a double take. Heels? Never before had Ms. Jenkins worn heels.

"Class, today we'll be working on still lifes. Please draw fruit or flowers." Ms. Jenkins's normally soft blue eyes grew hard as ice and she added, "And class . . . draw neatly, please." She looked at Ella in particular. Ella's face grew hot. She nodded and looked down at her sketchpad, conscious that Jamie still stared at her.

Never in her life had she wanted Jasper around more than now. She imagined his pink scarf and arched eyebrows; they would laugh their heads off at everything going on. She might have to wait until after school to talk to him, though. Right now she needed to just get through the day.

Ella began to draw, sketching a bowl of fruit under a vase of flowers. If Ms. Jenkins wanted neat, she'd give her neat. She hunched over and drew each line precisely. All of a sudden, she felt a presence behind her. She started and her pencil jerked, scratching a line through her entire drawing.

Ms. Jenkins was hovering close behind her. "Well, now you've ruined a perfectly good drawing!" She put her hand on Ella's shoulder and pressed down hard. "What do we have to do to make you draw neatly, Ella?"

Ella looked at Ms. Jenkins, eyes wide. The teacher stepped back and smiled, but her eyes remained hard. She narrowed them. "You're just quite the rebel, aren't you? I mean, look at your outfit! So revealing . . ."

Ella stood up and stammered, "I . . . don't . . . outfit?" Now the entire class stared at her. Ms. Jenkins came toward Ella, a wild look in her eyes. "Ella Ruby, in this class, we are neat!"

Ella backed up and bumped against the table. Ms. Jenkins kept coming toward her, and Ella began to shake. Was it possible Ms. Jenkins would do something to her? Why didn't any of the students do anything? She looked around the room. The others had smiles pasted on their faces, but their eyes were hungry and malicious.

Just then, the bell rang. The noise startled Ms. Jenkins, but the cold look didn't go out of her eyes. She raised an eyebrow at Ella and said, "Tomorrow, then." Ella grabbed her bag and ran out of the room before anyone else could say anything else to her.

11

Ella opened her locker door and stuck her upper half inside. Before she could get too comfortable and let the tears she'd been holding in all day fly, the door swung open again. Ella took a deep breath and clenched her fists. She would not hide anymore. She stood up straight, ready to face her attacker head-on.

"Goodness, are you having an *Alien vs. Predator* moment or what?" Jasper stood in front of her, a bemused smile on his face.

Ella threw her arms around him.

"I'm so glad . . ." she choked and sobbed. "Where have you been? Everyone . . . cardigans . . ."

Jasper patted her back and then moved away, his hands still on her shoulders. "Darling Ella, what's going on with you?"

Ella started to answer and then stopped. Her voice got hard. "Why are you wearing that?"

Jasper looked down at his outfit. He wore a pastel pink cardigan and jeans. "I felt it was a pink kind of day, like always." He put his hands on his hips and posed.

Ella shook her head. "So, there wasn't an announcement about cardigans or anything?"

Jasper shook his head. "No announcement, crazy girl. Why?" He looked around, and then his mouth made an O of surprise. "Whoa. What is going on?" A few students stared back at him.

Ella grabbed his arm. "It's way worse than yesterday, Jasper. Ms. Jenkins yelled at me in class and I think . . ." Jasper's eyes were wide. Ella lowered her voice. "I think she was going to hurt me."

He took a deep breath and looked around. "Are you sure? Ms. Jenkins? I can't believe she'd yell at you, let alone hurt you."

Ella said, "Do you think I'd make something like that up?" Her voice had risen. Students glared at her in passing. She lowered her voice to a whisper. "Jasper, something is horribly wrong here."

Just then, the hallway went quiet. Jasper and Ella looked up. At the end of the hall they saw Aaron Adler, one of the smallest freshmen, being surrounded by Carlos Perez and his friends.

Carlos, his hair combed neatly and his cardigan in place, said, "We don't believe you're exactly Bridgewater High material." Carlos towered over Aaron, and the rest of his friends stepped in closer. "I think you might be happier at St. Philomena's, don't you?"

Aaron didn't answer, but his teeth chattered. Ella and Jasper moved to help the poor kid. Before they could reach him, though, Carlos said, "Come on, let's go." He and his friends backed off. As they moved past their shaking victim, Carlos cocked his elbow and let a punch fly. Aaron crumpled to the ground.

Ella put her hands over her mouth. Aaron's nose was completely bloody. His right eye was already swelling and turning purple. "Are you OK?" Ella asked.

Aaron grabbed his bag out of his locker and slammed the door. He looked at them with his good eye and swiped the back of his hand under his nose. "No, I'm not OK. And neither are you! I'm getting out of here before they start killing us!" Aaron fled the hall. Jasper and Ella stood looking at each other.

"Carlos Perez is a jerk, but he's never been violent before," Ella said.

Jasper nodded. "Yeah, but he's never worn a cardigan before, either. Something tells me that Aaron just might be right. I think we're in real trouble here, Ella Ruby."

When Ella got to her locker the next day, a note had been taped to it. In neat penmanship, the note read: "We don't want you here."

The first bell rang, but Ella stayed where she was, waiting for Jasper.

Finally he showed up. Ella covered her mouth with her hands and gasped. His pink rugby shirt had grass stains on the front. His left eye was puffy and getting puffier by the minute. A cut on his lip bled deep red.

"What happened?" Ella shrieked. A few students glared at her, but she glared right back.

Jasper, with a shaky voice, said, "They jumped me outside the school. I didn't even see it coming."

Ella said, "Perez and his friends?"

Jasper shook his head and touched his lip. "No, the *drama club*!"

"What?"

Jasper nodded. "I know! I guess I should be thankful it wasn't the football team. The drama club can only throw fake punches." His face twisted in a smile, then he sucked in a quick breath. "Ow. Guess some were real."

Tears rushed to Ella's eyes. She couldn't believe the drama club would do this to him.

"That's it. We're going to the principal's office."

Jasper shook his head. "I don't want to be a snitch. Besides, it's not like the club is acting any different from the rest of the school. The weird thing is, they were so polite while they were beating me up. . . ."

Ella shook her note. "That's the point! I

think it's time Principal Meyer knew, don't you? You're not the only one who isn't welcome here. Look at this note." Jasper read it over, and his eyes grew wide.

"What is going on, Ella?"

"I don't know, Jasper. But we can't just wait to get attacked."

Jasper nodded grimly. "Agreed. To the principal's office."

The principal's secretary looked them up and down when they walked in. "You can't come in here dressed like that," she said. Her eyes lingered over Ella's jeans and Jasper's grass-stained rugby shirt.

"That's why we were sent here," Ella said quickly, "because of how we look."

The secretary nodded smugly. "As you should have been. Principal Meyer will deal with you in a moment."

Ella and Jasper shared a look.

After a few minutes, the door to Principal Meyer's office finally opened.

To Ella's surprise, Marta walked out, smelling of burnt sugar and cookies.

"What's she doing here?" Jasper whispered.

Ella wondered the same thing. Marta gave them the same disgusted look she'd had at their first meeting. Then she pasted on a smile.

"Hello, dears. Have a scrumptious day!" Her sleeveless yellow dress ruffled as she walked past.

Before Ella could think more about it, Principal Meyer stuck his head out the door and invited them into his office.

Ella had always liked Principal Meyer—he wasn't so bad for a principal. He was fair and could even be funny at some pep rallies. He twiddled his fingers in front of him. "Now, what can I do for you two?"

Ella breathed a sigh of relief. Finally. Someone who hadn't gone crazy. "Well, Jasper got beat up this morning by the drama club, and someone left this note for me," she said. She slid the note across the desk to the principal.

Principal Meyer read the note, then folded it carefully and set it down. "Well, this is indeed troubling."

Ella and Jasper nodded. Ella said, "I think it's getting worse, too."

The principal arched his eyebrows. "Worse than it already is?"

Ella and Jasper nodded again.

The principal sighed. "Well, I hope not. Your behavior is appalling as it is; any worse and I'll have to expel you." He looked pointedly at both Jasper and Ella.

Both of them sat stunned. Finally, Jasper spoke. "What now?"

Principal Meyer cleared his throat. "Here's what we'll do. You two go home for the day and think about what you've done to deserve this. I think the answer will come easily for you; just start by looking in the mirror. And then, if you can adjust your behavior appropriately, you may come back."

Ella couldn't move. The principal made a shooing motion. "Well, go! I'll have to speak with your parents, of course, but I hope this little talk will get you motivated. Go on, go!"

Jasper and Ella scrambled up and out of the office. As they passed the secretary, Ella heard her say under her breath, "Good riddance to bad rubbish!"

Ella and Jasper walked home on the backstreets. When it was time for Ella to turn down her block, Jasper stopped her.

"Be careful, *ma chérie*. I don't know what's happening, but I have a bad feeling that something even worse is coming."

Ella nodded. She felt the same way. "You too, OK? Juju?"

Jasper gave her a fierce hug. "Bees," he said and walked toward his house.

Ella turned and walked to her house. She

couldn't wait to tell her mom about the day—
Ella knew she'd be livid. Her ever-protective
mother would know what to do. Sara Ruby
always spoke her mind and always stood
up for what was right, even if it was often
embarrassing for Ella. Right now, Ella couldn't
think of a better mom to have.

Her door opened before she could turn the
handle, and her mom stood there, mostly in
shadow. "Ella May, come in here."

Ella knew that tone—she was in trouble.
Principal Meyer must have already called. She
knew, though, that once she told her side of
the story, her mom would see what was right.
"Mom, I want to tell my side," she said.

Her mom was quiet, but then opened the
door all the way and said, "Of course, dear."

As Ella stepped in she saw that her mom
wore a dress with a flouncy skirt, high heels,
and pearl earrings. Her mother never wore
dresses. Or pearls. Her mom pointed to the
couch and said, "We have a lot to talk about."

Shocked, Ella dropped her bag in the corner
and walked slowly to the couch. Her mom sat
down next to her, smoothing her skirt and sitting

with the straightest posture Ella had ever seen on her. Before her mom could speak, Ella started.

"Mom, someone beat up Jasper. And someone left a mean note on my locker. And then Principal Meyer blamed us! I think something huge is happening at the school—people are acting really... normal! But bad normal!"

Her mom nodded her head sadly. When Ella was through she said, "I know, dear. Your day sounds just dreadful."

Ella narrowed her eyes. "Why are you talking like that? And what are you wearing?"

Her mother touched a pearl earring and smiled. "So, of course you're grounded for the trouble you've caused. Oh, and I'm putting on a holiday party next week, but I think it best if you stayed in the basement the whole time. It just wouldn't do to have my friends see you, what with the way you look and behave!"

Tears sprang to Ella's eyes. She couldn't believe her own mother would say something like that to her.

Her mom stood up and smoothed her skirt down. "Now, go to your room and stay there."

She noticed Ella's expression and put her hand on Ella's shoulder. Looking down at her, she said, "Now, don't look so sad, dear. Would you like to take a cookie to your room?"

Ella looked to her left and saw half a package of Marta's cookies on the end table beside her, blue-and-white ribbon undone and cellophane crinkled. She picked up the package and stomped over to the garbage can, where she threw the cookies with all her might.

Her mother's eyes narrowed and her voice got hard. "Enough of this!" Her mom seized her arm and dragged her up the stairs to her room. She threw Ella like a rag doll onto the floor. Then she stopped in the doorway before she left. "You'd better learn how to behave, or things are going to get much, much worse." And then she slammed the door, leaving Ella shaking and bewildered on the floor.

Choking back sobs, Ella fumbled in her
pocket for her cell phone. She took it out
and hit speed dial for Jasper.

After two rings, he picked it up with a
whispered "Hello?"

Ella said through tears, "Jasper? My mom's
gone crazy."

Jasper whispered, "My parents are insane,
too. What is going on, Ella?" Never before had
Ella heard Jasper scared. Now he sounded
downright terrified.

"I don't know," Ella said. "Can you sneak out? Meet me downtown by the theater."

"Absolutely. I need some sanity. Juju."

"Bees." Ella hung up.

She wiped her eyes and put on her winter coat. Her boots were downstairs, so she had to put on regular shoes. She hoped they would give her enough traction to climb the trellis on the side of her house.

Creeping out her window, she managed to get a foothold on the first rung of the trellis and climb down without slipping too much. Through a side window she saw her mother dusting and humming, her big skirt silhouetted in the light. Ella fought back tears once again. She squared her shoulders, looked straight ahead, and sprinted all the way to Main Street, slipping once or twice without her boots.

Nearing downtown, Ella slowed down, afraid of what she'd find. All the women she passed wore fur coats with hats to match. All the men wore fedoras.

Looking across the street, she noticed a long, snaking line and wondered what everyone was waiting for. Sneaking forward, she got a look at the window. It was Marta's Bakeshop.

She caught a glimpse of bright pink out of the corner of her eye and whirled to face the theater. Jasper stood out in Technicolor glory, shifting back and forth in the cold. Ella's eyes went wide. He was a walking target in that pink.

Slouching along, Ella made it to him and pulled him to the other side of the theater. Her breath came out in white puffs.

Jasper yelled, "Ella! What are you doing? You scared the bejeezus out of me!"

Ella put her finger on his mouth. "Shh! Do you want to get us killed?"

Jasper moved her finger aside. "Killed? Good god, Ella, you should be in the drama club."

Ella dropped her arms to her side. "Are you kidding, Jasper? My mom just told me she wanted to keep me in the basement, and you think I'm being dramatic? She's wearing pearls, Jasper!"

Jasper snorted. "Sara in pearls. I'd love to see that. I'm not saying things aren't weird, I just don't know about the killing part, that's all."

Ella tried to be patient. "Jasper, things are bad. Really, really bad. And you come here in a neon sign that says 'come beat me up'?"

Jasper's mouth dropped open. "I'm sorry, are you saying I'm asking to be beat up?" He moved away from her.

Ella shook her head. "No! I'm just saying that right now's not the time to be so . . . out there, you know?"

Jasper looked at her coldly. "No. I don't know."

"You wear pink all the time—no guy does that! And you're loud, and you do voices, and you can be a little embarrassing! I mean, I lost the opportunity to work at that bakeshop because of you! Right now, we can't afford your . . ."

"My. What." Jasper punched each word. "Myself?"

Ella exhaled. This was coming out all wrong. "No! Your . . ."

Jasper's eyes were bright and shiny. "My personality. Who I am. You lost your job because of who I am, is that what you're saying?"

Ella's eyes filled with tears. "No, Jasper, I love who you are, just—"

"Just not around other people," he finished and began walking away. Stopping, he faced Ella. "You know, I expect other people not to understand. Lots of people are closed-minded. But my best friend? I thought *you* were different, Ella. Turns out you're just the same as everyone else."

Jasper turned around and left Ella standing there, tears streaming down her face.

When Ella woke up, her mom stood above her, spatula in one hand. "Wakey wakey, lazy lassie!" said her mom.

Ella sat up and rubbed her sore, puffy eyes. She remembered now why her eyes hurt so much. After she'd sneaked back into the house, she'd cried herself to sleep. The look on Jasper's face was burned into her memory; she'd devastated her best friend. Now her newly crazy mother stood over her, a manic look in her eyes. The smell of pancakes and sausage wafted through her bedroom door. Ella moved to get up.

Her mom smacked her leg with the spatula. A cold smile appeared on her face. "No, no dear. I'll bring you breakfast. What would our neighbors think if they saw you through the window?" She winked and smiled, then turned around on her heels. Ella heard a strange, metallic sliding noise outside her door, something that sounded suspiciously like a lock turning. Ella bounded up and tried to open the door.

Trapped. Her mom must have installed a lock outside her door while she slept. Ella put her back against the door and slid down. Cradling her legs, she put her head on her knees and cried some more. Her mother was lost. Everyone at school was ready to kill her. And now she'd driven Jasper away because she wasn't strong enough to stand by him. Her quest to be normal seemed so stupid now; what was life without her best friend? Who would be the bees to her jujus?

The door banged, and Ella scrambled away from it. Her mother entered and set a tray down by Ella's bed. The pancakes-and-sausage aroma filled the room. Ella's stomach growled, but she eyed the food suspiciously.

Her sort-of mother said, "Breakfast, dear." She popped around the other side of the door and came back in with two shopping bags. Putting one down, she opened the one in her hand and pulled out a pastel yellow cardigan, a long beige skirt, and a short-sleeved white blouse with ruffles. Then she pulled out yellow ballet flats.

"Some gifts for you, sweetie. We'll have to buy you more, as I've gotten rid of all your other clothes."

Ella gasped. "You what?"

"Well, they were just too inappropriate for such a young girl. In the other bag are some games to keep you occupied today and tonight. I'll be here all day, but tonight at seven o'clock is a town hall meeting, and I'm afraid I'll be leaving to attend. We'll be discussing what to do with those who aren't quite . . . fitting in, so it's very important I go."

Ella swallowed. "I have to stay in my room all day?"

Her sort-of mother patted her knee. "Just until you decide to wear these beautiful clothes." She smoothed Ella's hair. "And maybe put a little flip in this hair of yours."

Ella's eyes filled with tears again. With another pat on her knee, Ella's sort-of mom breezed out of her room.

The metal sliding sound jolted Ella into action. She'd sneak over to Jasper's. Then she'd make amends and . . . and what? Besides the fact that Jasper ignored all her texts and calls, and she had no idea what he'd do if she showed up at his house, what could she and Jasper do?

Ella thought that maybe a plan of action would help smooth things over with Jasper. He could never resist a clandestine operation—it was so much like acting. Then she had it: she'd go to the town hall meeting, wearing her new clothes to fit in. Really, they were maybe one step more conservative than what Ella normally wore. Then maybe she could figure out what was going on with everyone in town. Hopefully, Jasper would be there and would join in.

With the new plan, Ella felt stronger. Once she had Jasper back, she was pretty sure they could do anything.

At six thirty Ella pounded on her door and yelled, "Mother!"

Her sort-of mom opened the door to Ella in her brand-new outfit, her brown hair flipped neatly at the ends. Ella's mom went teary.

"Beautiful, dear, just beautiful." Her mom put on a pouty expression. "But now I'm going to the meeting."

Ella put on her best smile. "I was hoping to go to the meeting with you, Mother." She kept her eyes wide open and innocent.

Her mom put her finger to her mouth, then looked Ella up and down again. She exhaled. "All right, dear, but very best behavior, please."

"Yes, Mother. Best behavior, I promise." Ella had to fight the urge to retch.

Her mom winked at her, then pulled out a bit of cookie from a hidden pocket in her skirt. "Cookie?"

Ella gritted her teeth, pasted on a smile, and shook her head. "More for me!" her mom said, laughing. Ella had to fight the urge to roll her eyes. She so wished Jasper was here. She knew this would be the role of his lifetime.

Ella and her mom got into the car and drove to Bridgewater High, where the meeting would be taking place. Orderly lines of people streamed into the building, everyone in hats and heels, gloves, and coiffed hair. Murmurs of "How do you do?" "Fine night, isn't it?" and "Pardon me" filled the air.

She and her mom found seats in the last row of the auditorium. The place was eerie. Each person sat straight as a board and stared straight ahead. They all wore interested, bright expressions like inquisitive mannequins. Ella's mom leaned over to her and whispered, "Isn't that your friend Jasper, dear?"

Ella leaned forward. Three rows down was Jasper's head, his hair in a neat side part. He wore a tasteful sweater in beige—a color she thought he'd die before wearing . . . unless he was undercover like her. Her heart leapt. Of course he was undercover! They were best friends and thought alike. Her ally was only three rows down.

Principal Meyer came onto stage and introduced Mayor Wilkins. The auditorium was as silent as a graveyard.

"It has come to my attention that while our town is improving, we seem to have those who are less enthusiastic about fitting in. This meeting is to talk about how to persuade these people to try harder."

Ella noticed for the first time that Marta from Marta's Bakeshop was on the stage, sitting right next to Principal Meyer. She let a squeak of frustration slip, and her mom looked at her sharply. Ella turned the noise into a dainty cough. Her mom patted her knee and continued to pay attention.

Mayor Wilkins continued. "I propose instituting Difference Demerits for those who do not live up to our new code in Bridgewater. A first offense, or one demerit, will incur a warning, and a second offense, or two demerits,"—the auditorium silent—"will result in the death of the offender."

Ella nearly gasped. *Death?* Suddenly, the auditorium filled with applause. Wide-eyed, Ella looked at her mother, who applauded as loudly as anyone else. Mayor Wilkins smiled and said, "I will take that as a yes. Excellent. The new rules will be enforced immediately."

As the applause died down, Ella gulped. A lone hand rose up. Squinting, Ella could make out the back of Rash's head four rows down from Jasper. Her hair was unruly, her clothes baggy and worn-out. Ella's heart sank. This was not going to be good.

Mayor Wilkins shielded his eyes and asked in a bewildered voice, "Yes?"

Ella looked out at the crowd and saw how they all leaned toward Rash with menacing eyes.

Rash stood up. "Excuse m-m-e, Mr. Wilkins." Her face was bright red. "What exactly is a punishable offense?"

Mayor Wilkins looked surprised. Then he started to laugh. Soon all the people in the auditorium laughed with him. Ella pretended to laugh, too. She looked at Jasper and saw his shoulders shaking with laughter as well. She hoped he'd turn around and give her a secret look. But Jasper's gaze seemed to stay firmly on Rash.

Well, he *was* a very good actor.

The mayor wiped his eyes and said, "Young lady, that right there is one punishable offense. One demerit. Consider this your warning."

Ella's mom leaned into her and said, "I'm so very glad she is not my daughter. She won't last long here."

But Rash wasn't through. Ella stiffened in her seat as she heard the girl's voice ring out again. It took all her strength not to climb down the rows of chairs and put her hand over Rash's mouth.

Rash said, "But why? I'm just asking a question! How am I supposed to know what a punishable offense is?"

The audience seemed to gasp in unison. Mayor Wilkins stayed ramrod straight. With a glint in his eye, he leaned in close to the microphone.

He said quietly, "This girl has earned two Difference Demerits." Then he hissed, "Get her!"

Ella gasped. Rash looked around as a roar traveled through the audience. Ella's mother's eyes had gone black; her expression was both gleeful and ugly. The audience seemed to stand up as one and move toward Rash.

OK. It was time for her and Jasper to come out of hiding. They had to help this girl.

Ella stood up with the rest of the crowd and almost knocked over the person next to her. Ignoring her mother's calls, she elbowed her way through the sea of people, looking for

Jasper while keeping an eye on Rash. The mayor and Principal Meyer grabbed hold of Rash's arms, and Ella's stomach clenched. Terror filled Rash's eyes.

A chant rose up through the crowd. "Kill her, kill her, kill her . . ."

Ella felt sick. They were really going to do it. The mayor and principal moved Rash toward an exit near the stage. Ella continued to elbow her way through the crowd. She caught a glimpse of yellow tulle peeking out from behind the curtains, and she wondered again why Marta was here.

Then she saw them: the beautiful cowlick and the sweet eyes of her best friend. She pushed her way to him and pulled him to the side. "Jasper," she whispered, "I'm so glad to see you. What are we going to do? We have to help her!"

Confusion spread across his face. "Golly, Ella, whatever are you doing?"

Ella grunted in frustration. No one paid them any attention; the crowd was too busy trying to commit murder. He didn't need to act right now.

"Stop pretending, Jasper!" she whispered fiercely. "Nobody is paying any attention to us." Then Ella said what had been weighing on her since the night of their fight. "Jasper, I'm sorry for being such a jerk yesterday. I love who you are, just as you are." She leaned in closer. "I'm glad we had the same idea to go incognito. Now, how are we going to save Rash?"

Jasper's face had gone white. "Why ever would we save her?" He backed away from Ella. "And I believe that gives you one demerit."

Ella stared in disbelief. "Jasper?"

"Yes, Ella?" Jasper's eyes were cold. "Are you going to help dispose of Rachel or not?"

Tears rushed to her eyes and Ella swallowed, unable to speak.

Jasper grabbed her shoulders. Hard. "Well?"

Ella yanked away from him.

They had gotten to Jasper. They had taken her best friend.

Jasper stared at her, his eyes hard as marbles. Then a slow smile spread across his face. Ella could see the words forming on his mouth. "Two demerits."

Ella turned and ran through the crowd. She made her way to Rash's side just as the principal and mayor were walking her out the door.

Out of breath, she tried to think of a way to grab Rash and run before Jasper-who-wasn't-Jasper turned her in. Rash turned miserably toward Ella. It was all she could do to not grab her and run right there.

Smiling sweetly, Ella said, "Mr. Meyer, may I please walk with you? Rash and I were good friends, and now I want to help dispose of her."

Rash hiccupped a strangled sob. Ella ducked her head and pretended to cough. She managed a wink at Rash, who immediately grew quiet.

For an agonizing minute, Principal Meyer looked approvingly over Ella's outfit. "What a change! Very good. You are quite the success story."

Ella heard a rumbling through the crowd. She could hear murmurs of "Kill her too!" She knew they were meant for her. She forced herself to smile sweetly at the mayor. "May I have the honor of escorting her to her execution, sir?" Ella reached out her arms for Rash.

The mayor thought for a moment. The crowd grew louder and louder. Ella could hear her mom's and Jasper's voices above the fray. Any minute now, word would get to the mayor and the principal that she had two demerits. Ella blinked her eyes wide, looking as innocent as she could.

Finally the mayor said, "I think that's an excellent idea. Take her to the center of town. We'll do it there for everyone to see."

Meyer and Wilkins let go of Rash's arms.

Ella quickly yanked the stunned girl through the door. As the door shut behind them, she heard a wild, inhuman cry go through the crowd. She pulled Rash faster and they tripped down the street.

After two or three blocks, Ella looked over her shoulder and saw that no one was following them. They must have taken the time to put on their coats, since it wouldn't be proper to be seen without one. *A coat*, Ella thought as the cold caught up to her, *would be great about now*. Snow was coming down hard now, and the wind was picking up.

When they made it to a park on the outskirts of town, Ella turned to Rash, who was holding her sides and trying to catch her breath. Snowflakes froze on her eyelashes, and her eyes were open wide. "What . . . the hell . . . just happened in there?" she panted.

Ella shook her head. "Something's happened to our town."

Rash rolled her eyes. "Ya think?"

Ella chewed on her lip as she tried to work out a plan. She mentally took stock.

1. The people in the town had turned into crazy, cardigan-wearing murderers.
2. Her mother hated her.
3. And the clincher: she'd lost her best friend.

She made a decision and squared her shoulders. "I'm going back into town to find out why this is happening."

Rash's eyes got even wider. "Are you crazy? They'll kill you for sure!"

"Not if I don't get caught."

Rash stared in disbelief. "But why would you even try? Let's just get out of here!"

Ella shook her head firmly. "I may have been a little too worried about what people thought before. . . . And I may have tried my whole life to not get noticed. . . . But Rachel, when someone messes with my mom *and* my best friend, I have no problem diving into the mess to save them!" Ella stared hard at Rash and said from her gut, "I have to do something."

Rash decided that the best thing to do was to leave town. Ella helped her sneak back into her house and pack a few belongings. Then she waited with her at the bus stop.

"Are you sure you don't want to come?" Rash asked as the bus pulled up. Ella shook her head.

"Thanks. And good luck, Ella," Rash said, looking forlornly over her shoulder.

As the bus pulled away, Ella's mind spun. She headed into downtown Bridgewater.

With each stomp, Ella felt stronger and full of purpose. She could learn to color outside the lines if it meant saving Jasper and her mother.

When she reached Main Street, she stopped suddenly.

She realized she didn't have a plan.

Who could she run to? It seemed everyone had been at the meeting, including Sheriff Brady. The police wouldn't be of any help. *All* the so-called important town figures had been there, in fact. Who else could she run to? She mentally replayed the events at the high school.

Then, Ella stopped. It hit her with a shock— Marta. Somehow this all had to do with Marta. Why *had* she been sitting up on stage? Why had she been in Principal Meyer's office?

Ella needed answers, and the bakeshop was as good a place as any to start. She walked briskly through the cold and rounded the corner by Marta's Bakeshop. Then she stopped short: outside the beautifully decorated window, a long line snaked its way through the street, reaching almost to the theater.

She clenched her fists. Really? The cookies were that good?

And then, like a puzzle that finally came together, like jujus and bees, the answer clicked in her head.

It was the *cookies*.

It all made sense. Rash couldn't eat them because of her wheat allergy. And she and Jasper had boycotted them. And if she remembered right, Aaron Adler's family was strict about being Jewish—he probably didn't eat the cookies because they weren't kosher.

Ella thought back on the events of the last week. When the cookies appeared in the lunchroom—that's when everything started getting weird. Ella remembered Jamie walking in with no Mohawk, Ms. Jenkins and her tucked-in blouse. And her mother eating cookies nonstop. It all fit.

Then her heart sank. Jasper must have eaten a cookie, too. He'd been such a good friend; he'd resisted eating the cookies until she'd betrayed him. And now he was a zombie like the rest of the town.

But not for long. Ella needed to get into the bakeshop, stat. She had to find out what Marta was doing to the cookies.

lla crouched down and ran to the alley behind Marta's bakery. *The recipe is probably 2½ cups flour, 1 cup sugar, and 8 ounces **evil**,* she thought. Shivering in the night air, she ducked behind a dumpster.

The shop's back door was propped open. Warm air was streaming out and light shone on the snow. For a minute it seemed like no one was in the shop. Then a shadow darkened the door. Ella recognized the silhouette of a full skirt.

Marta.

The shadow grew larger. Ella ducked farther behind the dumpster and peeked around the corner, trying not to breathe out puffs of air. It was dark so she hoped Marta couldn't see her.

Marta stood in the door, wiping her face and breathing out into the cold air. Ella covered her mouth.

Marta stopped breathing for a second and cocked her head to the side. Ella tried not to gasp. Had Marta seen her? Marta squinted into the night where Ella hid. Ella froze.

After what felt like an eternity, Ella heard a faint mumble from the shop. Marta didn't say anything at first. Finally she yelled, "Coming!" With one last look in Ella's direction, Marta disappeared back into the shop. Ella let out her breath in one long exhale.

Crouch-walking to the doorway, Ella peeked around the doorjamb and saw Marta in the kitchen with a sheet full of cookies in her hands. In a singsong voice Marta chirped, "Who wants a fresh cookie?" She pushed through the double doors and disappeared into the front of the bakeshop.

The back was empty. Ella sneaked in.

The back room was as neat and tidy as the front, each ingredient sparkling and clean and in its proper place. On an island in the middle of the room Ella saw a bowl full of icing and a rack of different food colorings, including a fluorescent pink. *Jasper would have loved that color*, Ella thought. *What's Marta even doing with a color like that?* Looking closer, Ella saw that the food coloring was a package deal. She snickered. She imagined the horror Marta would feel at an empty spot in a package. No wonder she kept the bright pink.

A huge jar of tan powder sat next to the bowl. A new type of brown sugar? But why was it in a glass jar? Taking a peek at the double doors that led to the front of the shop, Ella saw the back of Marta's head through the oval window. Other people's heads came into view occasionally, and a constant murmur of voices hummed behind the door. Marta seemed to be serving cookies to some very eager customers, so Ella had time.

Unscrewing the lid on the jar, Ella opened it and licked her finger, sticking it into the mixture. She felt horrible—this violated so many health codes—but she told herself she was doing it for the greater good. Pulling her finger out, she smelled the mixture.

And recoiled.

It smelled burnt and rotten, like a combination of a campfire and a trash heap. Ella wiped the mixture off on her skirt.

Definitely not brown sugar. Turning the jar around, she found a neatly scripted label in the same handwriting as the Help Wanted sign she'd seen in the window.

Conformity Powder
Uses: To tidy up messy behavior and demeanor.
Warnings: May cause murderous rage and intolerance of difference. **Highly addictive**. WILL BECOME PERMANENT WITHOUT ANTIDOTE IN 10–15 DAYS.

Ella finally had an answer—Conformity Powder. This must be how Marta hooked everyone! How she had turned the entire town into murderous crazies, including Ella's mother.

How she had turned Ella's best friend into the same type of zombie.

Setting the jar down on the table, Ella spun around. She scanned the shelves for something that might be the antidote.

Suddenly, a cruel voice hissed in her ear. "What do you think you're doing in here, missy?"

Ella jumped. Marta stood in the doorway, cheeks flushed, hair slightly askew, and cookie sheet in her oven-mitted hands. Ella had never seen a more manic, angry look in anyone's eyes.

"I believe you have two demerits, little missy," Marta said evenly. "And you know what that means." Marta slammed the cookie sheet down on the kitchen counter and moved toward Ella. Ella grabbed the bright pink food coloring and held it over the icing.

"One more step and I will pinkify your icing!"

Marta gasped and covered her mouth. Slowly, she lowered her arms and smoothed her skirt. Her face twisted in an unnatural smile. "No need for that, dear. We're all friends here. Would you like a cookie? They're fresh out of the oven." She actually batted her eyelashes at Ella.

Ella shook her head and narrowed her eyes. "I know what you've been doing to the cookies! You're a monster!"

Marta's smile turned into a scowl. "A monster? I'm saving your town, little missy! Why do you think there is war and hate in the world? Because of all these differences! I'm eliminating them for the greater good!"

"You're eliminating *people*!" Ella shot back.

Marta smirked. "You can't make a cake without breaking a few eggs." Her face grew hard. "Go ahead, missy, and put that awful pink in the icing. I'll just make more. I'll throw it out, just like I'll be throwing you out!"

Marta lunged, and Ella squirted the pink coloring in her eyes. With a howl, Marta stumbled blindly, her arms outstretched. Ella ducked away, and Marta slipped on the bright pink puddle on the floor. Her legs flew up, and she fell with a loud *thwack*.

Panting, Ella leaned over Marta and saw she was still breathing. But the fall had knocked her out. Ella looked around to figure out what to do with her. She dragged Marta to a corner in the kitchen and tied her hands and legs with the straps of an apron. As an afterthought, she put an oven mitt in Marta's mouth.

Satisfied, Ella brushed her hands together and began searching for the antidote. She looked in cupboards and behind stacks of dishes, positive that Marta must have it somewhere. She knew that with Marta's sense of symmetry, she would never keep a magic powder without an antidote. Ella herself never would have, either.

It really was a shame she hadn't gotten that job. Ella snorted. No, not a shame—the woman was crazy. But, they both did seem to love orderliness. All Ella had to do was think about where she herself would put an antidote . . . in the open! She wouldn't hide it, not if the powder wasn't hidden. They needed to be side by side to be organized. Looking at the shelves around the kitchen, she saw an open spot, just about the size of a jar, and moved closer. Sure enough, a matching jar sat next to the open space. She pulled the jar from the shelf. It had no label, but this had to be the antidote.

Now all she had to do was bake a bunch of cookies with the antidote and get everyone to eat them.

Her heart sank. No way would that happen. They would know they weren't Marta's cookies and they wouldn't eat them. In fact, they'd kill her if they saw her. She couldn't imagine how she could ever convince them not to kill her, let alone eat cookies she'd baked.

A knock on the door startled Ella out of her thoughts. A voice from outside called, "So terribly sorry, Marta, but we were wondering if you have more cookies?" The person's voice had an edge to it, and a slight tremor ran through the sentence. Ella remembered the warning on the side of the powder jar: *highly addictive.* Maybe that could help her. The people outside needed to have the cookies; maybe they'd take them from her after all.

Time to bake. Using her best Marta voice, she called out, "Yes, dear. Very soon. In thirty minutes or so the new batch will be ready."

A collective groan sounded from outside the door. Ella knew she was pushing it. She had exactly thirty minutes to come up with the most perfect batch of cookies—and perfectly decorated—of her life.

Ella took a deep breath. Well, she'd always wanted to be a baker.

Rushing around the room, she grabbed the ingredients for sugar cookies from memory. She picked up the jar of antidote uncertainly. How much of this did she put in? She put a little on her finger and touched it to her tongue. It tasted like vanilla.

OK, she'd skip the vanilla and use the antidote instead. Except a lot more of it.

"That's not the antidote, you know." Marta

had come to and obviously managed to spit out the mitt from her mouth. She turned on her side and faced Ella from the floor. Marta's voice was low and even.

Ella said the first thing that came to mind. "You're crazy."

Marta chuckled a low, evil chuckle. A knock on the door sounded again, and a voice said from the other side, "Do be a dear and hurry up, will you, Marta?"

Ella frantically began measuring ingredients. Marta said, "No one will eat your cookies, you know. I could yell and have you put to death right now, but I think I'd rather watch you fail. You don't have the talent to bake a perfect cookie." Her laugh made Ella cringe.

"You aren't yelling because the Conformity Powder is right here, and your little minions might find that suspicious," Ella retorted. Still, sweat beaded on Ella's temples as she whipped her mixture in the bowl. She had no idea if she was right about the powder. And worse, she had no idea if she did have the talent to make the cookies right.

Marta continued, "I practiced for years to get the right recipe and the right, steady hand to decorate." Ella continued stirring, adding the antidote liberally to her mixture. Marta winced, as if she'd just felt a sudden pain. Softly, she said, "Don't you see? After my son . . . took his own life, I had to make sure nothing like that ever happened again!"

". . . Took his own life?" Ella gasped.

Marta's face streamed with tears. "He was different. Much like that friend of yours. So you see, I had to stop that from ever happening again. After his . . . accident, I traveled all over until I found the perfect combination of mind-altering ingredients."

Ella shook her head. "But your son wasn't wrong; other people were."

Marta's eyes glowed. "Don't you see? With no differences, no one gets hurt! It's *perfect.*"

Ella stomped over to Marta. She'd had enough of this crazy logic, this cowardice. She leaned down looked Marta directly in the eyes, "Sometimes life is messy," she said. Then she put the oven mitt over Marta's mouth and tied it in place with another apron.

Knocks sounded again. The crowd was getting restless. Ella rolled out the dough and began to cut out shapes with Martha's cookie cutters. She set the shapes on a cookie sheet, slid it into the oven, and started on the icing.

For the first time since the cookies appeared, Ella was glad they made people more polite—otherwise they would have broken down the door already. Finally, the oven dinged. Ella took the cookies out and started to decorate.

The pounding on the door got louder. Sweat trickled down Ella's back as she squeezed the pastry bag with as steady a hand as she could manage. Each line, each decoration had to be perfect, or the townspeople would know.

She had six more cookies in this batch to go. Now the pounding on the door was deafening. Ella could hear the angry murmurs: "Crikey, what's taking so long?" and "Goodness, I would very much like a cookie at this moment." The people were coming apart—the addiction was taking hold.

Finally the last cookie was decorated. The next batch was in the oven. It was time to see if the crowd would eat them. Ella grabbed hold of the cookie sheet with the decorated cookies, took a deep breath, and flung open the door.

The crowd was quiet for a moment; Ella fervently hoped the addiction to the cookies would be enough to stave them off. Ella saw Jasper and her mother standing directly in front.

Jasper's eyes took her in, and Ella smiled hopefully. Jasper turned to the crowd and said, "Kill her!"

The crowd surged forward.

"Please wait!" Ella yelled.

They stopped. *This group really is polite*, Ella thought.

Ella stumbled for words. "Uh, Marta is already going to kill me, but as part of my punishment, I have to hand out these cookies first."

The crowd mumbled, and Ella saw several people shrug. From the back of the shop, Mayor Wilkins said, "That makes perfect sense. Besides,

I could definitely use one of Marta's cookies about now."

Mumbles of agreement went through the crowd. Ella trembled and moved toward Jasper. "Cookie?"

Jasper leaned over the tray and picked one up. Ella held her breath as he raised it to his mouth. Then he stopped and looked again at the cookies. "Wait a minute," he said. He looked suspiciously at Ella.

Ella froze. This was it. She would be murdered by the entire town, and her best friend would be the one to turn her in.

Jasper moved to the side and then took out his wallet. "I need to pay you." He brought out a dollar and handed it to her. Then he took a bite of the cookie.

Ella exhaled and smiled. The rest of the crowd grabbed cookies and handed her change. Soon the batch was gone. Ella heard the ding from the oven that said the next cookies were ready to come out. She ran back to the kitchen and took the second batch out.

As she took off her oven mitts and got ready to decorate the second batch, she felt that something wasn't quite right. Turning toward the place where Marta was tied, she noticed two aprons and an oven mitt on the floor. Suddenly, Ella felt a smack against her head and she fell. Stars danced in front of her eyes.

When her vision cleared, Ella looked up to find Marta standing above her, a cookie sheet in her hands. Her once-perfect hair stood out in clumps, and her bright red face was contorted in an ugly expression. Marta's eyes blazed at Ella. "You've. Ruined. Everything." She raised the cookie sheet high overhead, and Ella put her hands up to ward off the blow.

Out of the corner of her eye, Ella saw blurry figure streak in. Next thing she knew, the figure had tackled Marta to the floor.

Jasper's voice reached Ella's ears. "Nobody hurts my best friend."

Ella's eyes filled with tears. Jasper was back.

Marta got up and grabbed a knife from the counter. Jasper moved to Ella and Ella scrambled up. They held on to each other.

"You kids have no idea what you're doing. And you!" Marta jabbed in Jasper's direction. "All the work I've done is for people like you!"

Jasper arched his eyebrows. "Excuse me? People like me?"

Ella stepped forward and put herself between Marta and Jasper. "I think she means fabulous, fantastic, flamboyant, and fearless people, Jasper." Ella turned and smiled at Jasper. "And utterly perfect just the way they are."

Suddenly, Marta lunged forward with the knife.

Pushing Ella aside, Jasper grabbed Marta's wrist just before the knife could stab Ella.

He squeezed Marta's wrist harder with each word: "Stay. Away. From. My. Best. Friend." Marta's face contorted in pain, and she dropped the knife.

Just then, the doors to the kitchen flew open and Ella's mom ran in. Ella braced herself to defend against her own mother. Her mom's eyes moved from Ella to Marta to Jasper, then finally to the knife on the floor.

"What is going on in here?"

Ella almost burst into tears. That was her mother's voice—her real mother's voice. Sara Ruby stepped in front of Jasper and Ella and spoke in a low growl. "You stay away from my daughter. And my honorary son."

More people burst through the doors, including Sheriff Brady. His hand hovered near his gun. He looked bewildered. "What's going on in here?"

Her face a violent mask, Marta yelled, "Seize them!"

Sheriff Brady looked at Marta and said, "Now, why would I do that? Perhaps if you calm down, ma'am, we can talk this out."

Marta's eyes went wild and a scream tore through her. She backed up, her eyes blazing and her hair getting wilder and wilder. She laughed maniacally. "Good luck from now on, you foolish town! I tried to offer you my help, but you didn't take it!" Then she turned on her heels and threw herself out the door.

Ella thought she'd never get that laugh out of her head.

asper turned to Ella. "The last thing I remember is our fight. And then I come in here and that maniac is standing over you with a cookie sheet. And that dress!"

Ella just laughed and threw her arms around him. "It's a long story."

"Well, *ma chérie*, you will be telling me this story right away. But for now, a more important question: Why am I wearing this hideous outfit?!"

Ella giggled. "That's part of the story."

Ella's mom walked over to the two of them and gave them a hug. "There must have been a gas leak or something, huh? I feel completely out of it. Who was that awful woman? And did she actually pull a knife on you?" She rubbed her eyes like she had just woken up. Then she looked down at herself. "Oh wow, what am I wearing?"

Ella stifled more giggling. But then Mayor Wilkins burst through the door. "Excuse me, but I believe many of us would like some cookies out there." He tipped his head to the side and looked at Ella. "Oh dear. I do believe we must put you to death."

Jasper, Sheriff Brady, and Sara Ruby all looked at the mayor with jaws open. Ella sighed, walked over to the mayor, and stuck a cookie in his mouth. "Try this first."

Ella's mom scrunched her eyebrows and looked at Ella. "Let me guess—this is one of those *long* stories."

Ella nodded. "Oh yeah. And I'll tell you after we finish up making these cookies."

Ella snuggled into Jasper on the couch, finishing up the last of the cookies she'd baked. Her mom shifted under the blanket on the chair across the room, finishing off her own cookie.

"Ella, these cookies were delicious. And I love how you decorated them!"

Ella smiled. She had made her new signature cookies—Crazy Cookies—with asymmetrical lines and random frosting. Sprinkles intersected with sugar crystals, and white and chocolate frosting swirled together. Each cookie was unique and delicious.

Jasper licked his fingers. "And you want to go shopping next week? I'm not sure who this new Ella is, but I think I like her."

Ella giggled and said, "And I don't think I'll clean the baking dishes until tomorrow."

Both her mom and Jasper fake-gasped. Her mom said, "I still don't understand what happened to all of your clothes."

Jasper chimed in, "All my clothes disappeared, too. I think a lot of strange things happened during the gas leak. Everyone in town seems like they had something weird happen."

Ella licked some frosting off her fingers. She smiled a private smile and said, "Yeah, that gas leak was something."

Her mom stood up from her chair. "Well, I for one am glad things are getting back to normal. I don't know what's going on lately, but I do know that I'm ready for some stability."

Jasper stood up and put the back of his hand to his forehead. He said in his Southern-belle voice, "Why, Ms. Ruby, some normalcy is just what we need, don't you think?"

Ella smiled. Yep, she was glad things were back to normal, too. Even if they got a little messy once in a while.

Everything's fine in Bridgewater. Really . . .

Or is it?

Look for all the titles from the
Night Fall collection.

THE CLUB

Bored after school, Josh and his friends decide to try out an old board game. The group chuckles at Black Magic's promises of good fortune. But when their luck starts skyrocketing—and horror strikes their enemies—the game stops being funny. How can Josh stop what he's unleashed? Answers lie in an old diary—but ending the game may be deadlier than any curse.

THE COMBINATION

Dante only thinks about football. Miranda's worried about applying to college. Neither one wants to worry about a locker combination too. But they'll have to learn their combos fast—if they want to survive. Dante discovers that an insane architect designed St. Philomena High, and he's made the school into a doomsday machine. If too many kids miss their combinations, no one gets out alive.

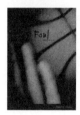

FOUL

Rhino is one of Bridgewater best basketball players—except when it comes to making free throws. It's not a big deal, until he begins receiving strange threats. If Rhino can't make his shots at the free throw line, someone will start hurting the people around him. Everyone's a suspect: a college recruiter, Rhino's jealous best friend, and the father Rhino never knew—who recently escaped from prison.

LAST DESSERTS

Ella loves to practice designs for the bakery she'll someday own. She's also one of the few people not to try the cookies and cakes made by a mysterious new baker. Soon the people who ate the baker's treats start acting oddly, and Ella wonders if the cookies are to blame. Can her baking skills help her save her best friend—and herself?

THE LATE BUS

Lamar takes the "late bus" home from school after practice each day. After the bus's beloved driver passes away, Lamar begins to see strange things—demonic figures, preparing to attack the bus. Soon he learns the demons are after Mr. Rumble, the freaky new bus driver. Can Lamar rescue his fellow passengers, or will Rumble's past come back to destroy them all?

LOCK-IN

The Fresh Start Lock-In was supposed to bring the students of Bridgewater closer together. Jackie didn't think it would work, but she didn't think she'd have to fight for her life, either. A group of outsider kids who like to play werewolf might not be playing anymore. Will Jackie and her brother escape Bridgewater High before morning? Or will a pack of crazed students take them down?

MESSAGES FROM BEYOND

Some guy named Ethan has been texting Cassie. He seems to know all about her—but she can't place him. Cassie thinks one of her friends is punking her. But she can't ignore how Ethan looks just like the guy in her nightmares. The search for Ethan draws her into a struggle for her life. Will Cassie be able to break free from her mysterious stalker?

THE PRANK

Pranks make Jordan nervous. But when a group of popular kids invite her along on a series of practical jokes, she doesn't turn them down. As the pranks begin to go horribly wrong, Jordan and her crush Charlie work to discover the cause of the accidents. Is the spirit of a prank victim who died twenty years earlier to blame? And can Jordan stop the final prank, or will the haunting continue?

THE PROTECTORS

Luke's life has never been "normal." His mother holds
séances and his crazy stepfather works as Bridgewater's
mortician. But living in a funeral home never bothered
Luke—until his mom's accident. Then the bodies in the
funeral home start delivering messages to him, and Luke
is certain he's going nuts. When they start offering clues
to his mother's death, he has no choice but to listen.

SKIN

It looks like a pizza exploded on Nick Barry's face. But a
bad rash is the least of his problems. Something sinister
is living underneath Nick's skin. Where did it come
from? What does it want? With the help of a dead kid's
diary, Nick slowly learns the answers. But there's still one
question he must face: how do you destroy an evil that's
inside you?

THAW

A storm caused a major power outage in Bridgewater.
Now a project at the Institute for Cryogenic
Experimentation is ruined, and the thawed-out bodies
of twenty-seven federal inmates are missing. At first,
Dani didn't think much of the news. Then her best friend
Jake disappeared. To get him back, Dani must enter a
dangerous alternate reality where a defrosted inmate is
beginning to act like a god.

UNTHINKABLE

Omar Phillips is Bridgewater High's favorite local teen
author. His Facebook fans can't wait for his next horror
story. But lately Omar's imagination has turned against
him. Horrifying visions of death and destruction come at
him with wide-screen intensity. The only way to stop the
visions is to write them down. Until they start coming
true . . .

SOUTHSIDE HIGH

ARE YOU A
SURVIVOR?

Check out all the books in the

SURVIVING SOUTH SIDE

collection.

Bad Deal

Fish hates taking his ADHD meds. They help him concentrate, but they also make him feel weird. When a cute girl needs a boost to study for tests, Fish offers her a pill. Soon more kids want pills, and Fish likes the profits. To keep from running out, Fish finds a doctor who sells phony prescriptions. After the doctor is arrested, Fish decides to tell the truth. But will that cost him his friends?

Beaten

Paige is a cheerleader. Ty's a football star. They seem like the perfect couple. But when they have their first fight, Ty scares Paige with his anger. Then after losing a game, Ty goes ballistic and hits Paige. Ty is arrested for assault, but Paige still secretly meets up with him. What's worse—flinching every time your boyfriend gets angry, or being alone?

Benito Runs

Benito's father has been in Iraq for over a year. When he returns, Benito's family life is not the same. Dad suffers from PTSD—post-traumatic stress disorder— and yells constantly. Benito can't handle seeing his dad so crazy, so he decides to run away. Will Benny find a new life? Or will he learn how to deal with his dad— through good times and bad?

PLAN B

Lucy has her life planned: she'll graduate high school and join her boyfriend at college in Austin. She'll become a Spanish teacher and of course they'll get married. So there's no reason to wait to sleep together, right? They try to be careful, but Lucy gets pregnant. Lucy's plan is gone. How will she make the most difficult decision of her life?

RECRUITED

Kadeem is Southside High's star quarterback. College scouts are seeking him out. One recruiter even introduces him to a college cheerleader and gives him money to have a good time. But then officials start to investigate illegal recruiting. Will Kadeem decide to help their investigation, though it means the end of the good times? What will it do to his chances of playing in college?

SHATTERED STAR

Cassie is the best singer at Southside. She dreams of being famous. Cassie skips school to try out for a national talent competition. But her hopes sink when she sees the line. Then a talent agent shows up and tells Cassie she has "the look" he wants. Soon she is lying and missing glee club rehearsal to meet with him. And he's asking her for more each time. How far will Cassie go for her shot at fame?